Saturday Night Date

by
Jane McManus

Watermill Press

Printed in the United States of America

Illustrations by Cat Calhoun

ISBN 0-89375-778-0

Contents

The Biggest Dance of the Year

"Gail, next Saturday night is the biggest dance of the year. You have *got* to tell your parents about it," Martha said.

"No, I can't do that," Gail answered her friend as they walked down the hall toward their history class.

"Larry's going to ask somebody else to the dance if you don't go with him," Martha exclaimed. "You know what might happen then."

"Yes, I know very well," Gail said softly. She had been thinking about it and worrying a lot. "He might like the girl he takes to the dance and not like me anymore."

"Well, do you want that to happen?" Martha questioned, upset.

"Of course I don't," Gail replied.

"Then you've got to tell your parents you can't work at the restaurant that night. You work too much anyway. You never go out with the rest of us anymore," Martha said. She was worried about her friend.

Crowds of students hurried past Martha and Gail, but the two girls were so wrapped up in their conversation that they just stood in the middle of the hall and talked.

"I can't tell my parents about the dance," Gail said sadly. "My father won't even be out of the hospital until Saturday morning." Gail tried to tell herself that it wouldn't always be this way, that she wouldn't always have to work so hard. "My mother has been working in the restaurant every day and every night," she told Martha. "I just have to work on Saturday so she can stay home with Dad and maybe get a little rest herself."

Just then, Larry came up behind them in the hall. "Hi, Gail. Hi, Martha," he said.

"Hi, Larry," they answered.

"Uh . . . Gail, would you go to the dance with me?" he asked.

Gail shook her head. It was hard for

7

"Now you've done it," Martha said:
"He's going to ask somebody else."

her to answer. "I'd love to go with you, Larry, but I just can't," she said. "I have to work that night."

Larry had a strange expression on his face. He looked disappointed and puzzled and hurt all at the same time. "Well, that's too bad," he said. "I'm sorry." Then he turned and hurried off to class.

"Now you've done it," Martha said. "He's going to ask somebody else. Maybe he'll even ask that flirt, Kara."

"I know," Gail answered. She tried to keep back the tears, but some rolled down her cheeks. Just then, the bell rang for the next class. Gail wiped her tears away quickly, and she and Martha hurried into the classroom.

After that, Gail didn't see Larry for several days. He didn't leave any notes for her in her desk in homeroom, and he didn't call her on the phone.

9

He doesn't like me anymore, she thought, *and I like him so much. Oh, I feel terrible!* Gail tried not to look as sad as she felt because she didn't want her mother to know about it. *Mom's got enough to worry about without worrying about me, too,* Gail said to herself. She held her head up high and tried to smile, but it wasn't easy.

At school, all of her friends talked about what they were going to wear to the big dance. Gail didn't want to hear about the dance. She was afraid she would hear that Larry had asked Kara to go with him.

Two days before the dance, Gail saw Larry in the hall near her history class. "Hi, Gail," he said. "I heard your father will be coming home from the hospital this Saturday. How is he?"

"He's getting a little bit stronger. We

think he'll improve a lot when he gets home," Gail answered. "How are you? I haven't seen you lately."

"Oh, I'm OK, I guess," Larry answered. His face looked sad though. "Well, I've got to go to class," he said. He hurried off down the hall.

I don't know whether it's better to see him or not to see him, Gail thought. *I feel awful either way because I know he doesn't like me anymore.* She walked sadly into her history class.

On the night of the big dance, Gail went to the restaurant to work. She thought of her friends getting all dressed up and leaving for the dance with their boyfriends. She cleared off the counter and took two people's orders for ice cream and coffee. Her feet hurt already, and she felt very tired, but she didn't know why. She imagined Larry taking

Kara to the dance. She thought of how pretty Kara would look and how handsome Larry would be. Her heart ached.

As she was putting some dishes away, she heard someone else come into the restaurant. She turned around to take the order. It was Larry!

"Hi, Gail," he said with a little smile on his face.

"Hi, Larry," Gail said, her eyes lighting up. "I was just thinking about you."

"I hope you were thinking nice things about me," Larry answered shyly.

"Well, as a matter of fact," Gail said slowly, "I was thinking of you taking Kara to the big dance."

"I had thought about doing that," Larry said. "But I didn't really want to take her to the dance. I wanted to take you."

"And I wanted to go with you, too,"

Gail answered.

"Did you? I wasn't completely sure about that," Larry said.

"Oh, yes, more than anything!" Gail cried. "But I just had to work so my mother could stay home with my dad and get some rest."

"Well then, do you mind if I spend the evening here with you?" Larry asked.

Gail leaned across the counter and kissed him on the cheek. Suddenly, her feet didn't hurt, and she didn't feel tired anymore.

"We can talk when you're not too busy. Maybe I could even help you if a lot of people come in," Larry offered.

"I'd like that," Gail said happily.

Larry took her hand. "I would, too," he said. They smiled at one another.

"Would you two lovebirds excuse me?" came a cheerful voice from the end of

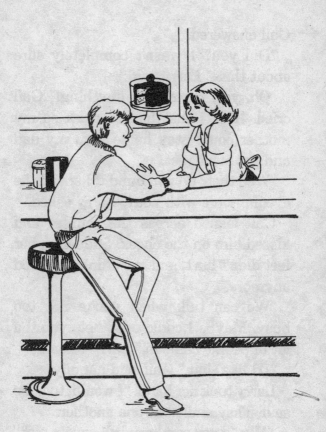

Larry took Gail's hand.

the counter. "I'd like a cup of coffee."

Larry and Gail started to laugh. "This is going to be a wonderful Saturday night," Gail said as she went to wait on the customer.

"One of the best," Larry answered. "Dance or no dance, I can tell it will be one of the best."

The Pen Pal

"Dear Pen Pal...Dear Bill." Debby chewed at the end of her pen. *This has to be a good letter. I want Bill to be my pen pal.*

I guess "Dear Bill" sounds best, she thought. Then she wrote, "My name is Debby Adams. I saw your name in *Pen Pal Magazine.*"

I guess "Dear Bill" sounds best,
Debby thought.

Debby got up and paced around the room. She looked at herself in the mirror and frowned. Then she walked back to her desk.

"I'm a freshman at Windsor High School," she started writing again. "My favorite subject is math. My hobby is taking photographs. I like to make new friends."

"Yeah!" Debby said out loud. "I make lots of new friends, but they're all girls."

Most of Debby's friends had boyfriends, but every time Debby tried to talk with a boy, she froze. She blushed and stumbled over her words. *Well, Bill won't ever know what I look like,* Debby thought.

She addressed the letter and mailed it. Then she started to get nervous. *What if he doesn't like me?* she worried. *What if he gets letters from pretty girls and doesn't want to write to me?*

Debby hurried home from school every day to check the mail. Finally, a letter came. Debby was excited as she opened it.

"Dear Debby," it started. "I would like to be your pen pal." A big grin spread across her face. "I am a junior at Hampden High," the letter continued. "I'm on the debating team, and I play basketball. My favorite subject is history, but I like math, too. Tell me about taking photographs. That must be fun! Your pen pal, Bill."

Debby read Bill's letter over and over again. She could hardly believe it was real!

That night, Debby wrote to Bill. She told him about her school's basketball team and about taking pictures for the school newspaper. She asked him about the debating team. She wondered whether he got nervous talking in front of a lot of people.

Five days later, Debby got another letter from Bill with a picture from his school paper. The picture showed Bill in a basketball uniform, jumping to make a basket.

"Oh, he's so good-looking," Debby cried, staring at the picture. "He won't like me at all!"

Bill's letter said, "I enjoy hearing from you. Taking photographs for the school paper must be exciting. Here's one of me that was just in our paper. The picture's not bad, but I missed the basket. I'd like to see some of the pictures you've taken. I'd like to see a picture of you, too."

"Oh, no!" Debby exclaimed. "He won't want to write to me again if he sees my picture." She paced around her room.

HAMPDEN HIGH

Hampden High team mate Bill
tries for basket in last
of game Friday

*The picture showed Bill in
a basketball uniform.*

Maybe I should send him a picture of somebody else, she thought. *Somebody cute. He'd never know.*

No, I can't do that, she decided. Then she got an idea. *I'll send him that crazy picture of me taking a picture of somebody else. The camera blocks most of my face.*

That night, Debby wrote to Bill. She tried to sound casual. She told him about a funny old movie she'd seen and asked him about his debate team. She told him she liked the picture he'd sent, and she sent him the crazy picture of herself with the camera in front of her face.

Well, I probably won't hear from him again, she thought sadly as she went to mail her letter.

But, by the end of the week, there was another letter. "No fair, Debby," it began. "That's a great picture of you with the camera. I wanted to see your smiling face, though."

Debby smiled when she read that. Then, as she read the next paragraph in the letter, her face got pale. "On Tuesday," the letter said, "I'll get a chance to see that smile in person. Hampden's Debate Team is traveling to the Mid-State Debate at your high school. I'm really looking forward to seeing you!"

"Well, that's it for sure," Debby said. "I have to take pictures of the debates, but I can't keep my camera in front of my face all day. He's going to see what I look like."

As the day of the debate got closer, Debby became more and more nervous. *He's so handsome,* she thought. *Maybe I should pretend I'm sick and not go to school that day.*

But, by the morning of the debate, Debby had decided to take a chance that Bill might like her. She washed her hair and put on her best jeans and her new pink shirt. She smoothed a little make-up on her cheeks and tried to smile at herself in the mirror.

As she walked into the auditorium carrying her camera, she felt numb. She looked up at the debate teams on the stage and immediately saw Bill. He was even more handsome than in his picture. Debby was about to run away when the photography advisor called, "Go down front, Debby. Get some close-ups of all the teams."

Debby headed down the center aisle of the auditorium. She saw Bill looking around at the audience. When he saw her with her camera, he smiled and tilted his head as if to ask who she was.

She smiled back and waved shyly. He nodded his head and smiled again in greeting.

Debby's heart was pounding. *He smiled at me,* she kept repeating to herself. She took several pictures of the debate teams without even thinking about what she was doing. Then she walked to the side of the auditorium to listen to the debates. She could hardly stand still, she was so excited. *He looked right at me, and he still smiled,* she thought.

When the debates were over, Bill hurried through the audience to Debby. "I'm glad you were here," he said. "Knowing I had a friend in this room full of strangers helped me win the debate."

"You were terrific. Congratulations!" Debby said. "Say, you should be celebrating."

Debby smiled back and waved shyly.

"Well, maybe I could convince a certain girl I know to celebrate with me over a pizza," Bill smiled warmly.

"You talked me into it," said Debby. And as they left the auditorium, she added with a laugh, "I guess we're not just pen pals anymore."

The Birthday Party

"Let's see," Penny said to her mother. "I want to invite Kate and David. And I'd like to ask Pam, which means I should invite Kevin, too, because she likes him."

"That's all right, honey," her mother

answered with a smile. "It's not every day that you have a sweet sixteen party. I think we can fit twelve people in the apartment."

Penny was adding up the names she had written on her list. "That's twelve," she said. "Plus Mike and me. Can we fit fourteen?"

"We'll squeeze you in somehow, birthday girl," her mother laughed.

"And Mike, too. I wouldn't want a party without him," Penny replied.

"How is Mike?" her mother asked. "I haven't seen him much lately."

"He's been busy and worried about school," Penny answered.

"Oh," her mother said thoughtfully. "Well, I hope everything is all right. Now, you should send out those invitations. Your birthday isn't that far away."

"We'll squeeze you in somehow, birthday girl,"
Penny's mother laughed.

Penny started to write her invitations. *It will be an exciting party,* she thought. She imagined herself dancing with Mike. *He's been my boyfriend for a long time, but he* has *been a bit moody lately.*

The next morning, Penny mailed her invitations on her way to school. *I can't wait for my party,* she thought. *It will be so much fun!*

When her friends got their invitations, they were almost as excited about the party as Penny was. But Mike didn't say anything at all about it. In fact, he seemed to be avoiding Penny. *I'm going to wait for him after baseball practice today,* she decided to herself. *I wonder if there's anything wrong.*

That afternoon, Penny got home late. Her nose was red, and her eyes were swollen.

"Penny, what in the world is wrong?" her mother exclaimed.

"Mike doesn't want to go out with me anymore. He doesn't even want to come to my birthday party," Penny said. She started to cry again.

"Oh, dear," her mother said sadly, taking Penny in her arms. "I'm so sorry, Penny."

"He wants to go out with that new girl, Roxanne. I feel so miserable," she moaned. "I'm going to have to cancel the party."

"No, dear," her mother said, "you can't do that."

Penny looked up, startled. "I *can't* have the party without Mike. Everybody else will be there *with* somebody. I don't want to sit alone in a corner at my own birthday party!" Penny cried.

"I don't blame you," her mother

answered. "But you can invite another boy. You can also try to enjoy yourself with your other friends."

"There aren't any other boys to ask," Penny complained. "All the nice boys I know already have girlfriends. Oh, I don't ever want to be sixteen," she cried. "It was a terrible idea to have a party!" She ran to her room, crying.

About an hour later, Penny came out to the living room. She had washed her face, and her eyes looked less puffy. "I'm sorry I got so upset," Penny said to her mother. "I'll have the party. Everybody's looking forward to it. You're right. It wouldn't be fair to cancel out now."

"I'm very proud of you, Penny," her mother said. "Not many girls are as mature at sixteen as you are."

Penny smiled sadly at her mother.

"I can imagine how you feel," her

mother said. "You've been going out with Mike for a long time."

"Two years," Penny said, nodding her head. Tears started to come to her eyes again.

"You'll probably feel sad for a while," her mother said softly.

"Forever!" Penny cried. Tears were rolling down her cheeks now.

Penny's mother nodded her head, remembering the feeling. "You won't always feel this way. It will hurt less and less as time passes," her mother said.

"That's hard to believe," Penny responded.

"I know it is, but it's true," her mother told her, "and something good may even come out of it."

"I don't think so," Penny said, wiping away her tears.

"Well, we'll see," said her mother.

Just then, the phone rang. Penny's mother answered it. "It's Kate," she said. "Do you want to talk now?"

Penny nodded her head. "Hi, Kate," she said, taking the phone. "What's up?"

"I'd like to ask you a favor, Penny," Kate said. "My cousin Sandy is moving to town the day of your birthday party."

"Yes?" Penny asked.

"Well, I wondered if I could bring Sandy to your party," Kate inquired.

Penny hesitated. *That will make one more girl without a date,* she thought. *Oh well, Sandy and I can sit together in the corner.*

"Sure, that's OK, Kate," Penny said. "Sandy can come to the party."

"Thanks, Penny," Kate answered. "You're a great friend! Good-by."

At first, Penny was worried that she

had made everything worse by saying Sandy could come. But on the night of the party, Penny was glad Sandy would be there. *At least I'll have somebody to talk to when everybody else is dancing,* she thought sadly as she finished getting ready.

"There's the doorbell, Penny," her mother called. "Put a big smile on that pretty face, and answer the door."

It was Maria and Paul. "Happy birthday!" they said, handing her some gifts. Then Juan and Ginny came, followed by Cynthia, Andy, Mark, and Patty. Everyone seemed to be in such a good mood.

Then the doorbell rang again. "That must be Kate and David and Sandy," Penny said. She opened the door. But to Penny's surprise, Kate, David, and a nice-looking boy with sandy-colored hair smiled back at her. "Oh . . . Sandy

Penny opened the door.

. . . I thought Sandy was a girl," Penny laughed.

"Sorry about that," Sandy said with a grin. "May I still come to the party?"

"Of course," Penny said. "Come in. I'm glad you could be here, and I'm glad that you're not a girl," she laughed again.

"So am I," he said, smiling at her.

Penny introduced Sandy to all her friends. Then he asked her to dance. It felt strange dancing with somebody other than Mike, but it was also exciting.

Sandy and Penny danced together a lot that evening. When they weren't dancing, they talked. By the end of the party, Penny felt as if she and Sandy had known each other for a long time.

"It's been a wonderful party," Sandy told Penny as they walked to the door.

"Yes, it has," Penny answered, "because you've been here."

Sandy gave Penny a quick kiss. "Happy birthday," he said. "I'll call you tomorrow, OK?"

"OK," Penny said, putting her hand on her cheek where he had kissed her.

He smiled and went down the hall with Kate and David.

Well, Penny said to herself as she watched Sandy go, *this has been a happy birthday after all.*

The Marathon

Steve had been training for the marathon for months. Now there were two weeks left before the twenty-six-mile race, and he was running hard. He had cut back on his homework and stopped seeing his friends. Dating girls was out of the question. But last week, Peggy

Callahan moved to town. Peggy was about the prettiest girl Steve had ever seen.

By the time I finish the marathon, Steve thought, *some other guy will be dating her.*

Steve ran into the park. Yesterday, he thought he had caught a glimpse of Peggy there. She had been dressed as if she were going to play tennis. Steve thought about running around the tennis courts a couple of times to see if she was there today. In fact, he thought about running around the tennis courts for the whole afternoon, but decided that would be too obvious.

There she is, he said to himself. *And she's not playing tennis. She's running! My dream come true—a gorgeous girl who runs!* Steve sprinted ahead to catch up with her. His heart was beating faster, and he knew it wasn't just from running.

"Hi, Peggy," he said as he came up behind her. She turned her head in surprise.

"Hi! You're Steve Wolansky, aren't you?" she asked as they ran side by side.

Steve was surprised. "I didn't think you'd know my name," he said.

"Oh, I know your name. You're special. You're training for the marathon, too," Peggy answered.

Steve could feel himself blush. *Special. She said I was special,* he thought. That made him feel as if he could run twenty-six miles backwards. Suddenly, the rest of what she said hit him. "Too?" he asked.

"Yes, I am, too—or I was anyway," she answered. "I'm just about to give up on it for this year. I had to break training when my family moved. I'm not running the way I should be at this point."

They turned off the main path and ran toward the pond. "I'm off my schedule, too," Steve said. "Maybe we could help each other. How many miles a day are you doing?"

"Ten," she answered, sounding very discouraged.

"You can still do it," Steve said. "Let's run together today and get to know one another. It should make the miles go by pretty easily."

"That sounds wonderful, Steve!" Peggy answered. Her dark blue eyes sparkled with excitement. "I'd like to learn some good trails, too."

"Let's go this way then," he said. They ran together on the trail through the woods and talked. By the end of ten miles, Steve was thinking, *I really like this girl!*

"You've got a good strong pace," he

told her. "You can finish the marathon this year."

"Do you really think I can?" she asked. "I want to so badly."

"I'm sure you can," Steve answered. He was surprised at how much he wanted to encourage Peggy.

"Well, I believe it then," she said happily. "If you say so, I believe it."

Just then, Steve gave a cry of pain. His right leg came up sharply, and he fell to the ground.

"Steve!" Peggy cried. "What's wrong?"

"My foot," he said, his face twisted with pain.

"Oh, no!" she cried, looking at his foot. "A piece of broken glass is stuck in your foot. I'm going to get help. Don't move."

Peggy ran faster than she had ever run in her life. All she could think of was the blood starting to color the cloth part of Steve's running shoes. She ran to the first house outside of the park. From there, she called for an ambulance and then raced back. By the time she reached the park, the ambulance had arrived. She led the people with the stretcher to the place where Steve was lying on the ground.

At the hospital, Steve had to have fifteen stitches. His foot was bandaged, and he was on crutches. Peggy stayed with him the whole time, holding his hand. When the doctor told Steve he couldn't run in the marathon this year, Peggy was the one who cried.

"Don't worry, Peggy," Steve said when he saw how sad she was for him. "I'm all right. I can do it next year. This year, you'll have to run for both of us."

"I can't now," she said. "Not after this!"

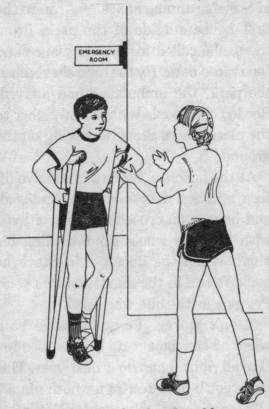

Steve's foot was bandaged, and he was on crutches.

"Yes, you can," he told her. "I *know* you can do it! Don't prove me wrong."

Every day after Steve's accident, Peggy trained hard. As she ran, she imagined Steve's voice saying, "I know you can do it! Don't prove me wrong."

Every night, Peggy and Steve talked on the phone. She wanted to know how his foot was — and to cheer him up. He would ask how her running was going. They both looked forward to these calls.

On the morning of the marathon, Steve went to Peggy's house early. "I'm so nervous, Steve," she said when she saw him. "I've never run twenty-six miles before. I'm crazy even to be trying."

"No, you're not," he said with a smile. "You've trained for a long time, and you're ready. In fact," he continued, handing her a little box, "I'm so sure you're going to finish that I brought you a victory gift."

She took a thin silver chain out of the box. "It's a bracelet," he said. "Wear it today for me."

"Oh, Steve," Peggy exclaimed, "I knew you were special! You haven't complained once about not being able to run yourself, and you've been so great to me. I really like you a lot!" She leaned forward and kissed him.

"I'm glad!" he said with a big smile. "Now you'd better get going. Look for me at the thirteen-mile mark. I'll be there. And I'll be at the finish line, too." He wished her good luck as he left.

Later, as Steve watched the runners pass the halfway point, he felt depressed. *I could have been there,* he thought.

Then Peggy came into view. She was running well and did not seem tired at all. She smiled when she saw him and

*Peggy was running well and did not seem
tired at all.*

pointed to the bracelet on her arm.

"You're doing great!" Steve yelled from the side of the road. All of a sudden, he didn't feel bad anymore.

Two hours later, he was waiting at the finish line when Peggy came up the last hill. She looked very proud to have made it to the end. Steve felt proud and happy as she ran across the finish line.

Peggy didn't stop running until she made it through the crowd and into his arms. "We won!" she said. "We won!" Then she started to laugh and cry at the same time.

"Yes, we did, Peggy," Steve said, still holding her. "We won!"

Too Many Dates

"Hey, Mom, look at this advice column in the paper," Ginny exclaimed. "It says teenagers shouldn't go steady until they're older. I wish I had that problem."

"It sounds like reasonable advice to me," Mrs. Scott answered, looking up from her book.

"Well, I'm not going steady," Ginny said unhappily. "I'm not even going out, but the paper doesn't say anything about that!"

"You will soon enough, dear," Mrs. Scott said. She put her book away. "Some day soon, you'll have too many dates—more than you know what to do with."

"I'd settle for just one at this point," Ginny complained. "Do you realize I've never had a 'real' date?"

"You went to the Mancusos' party with Tod last week," her mother reminded her.

"That doesn't count," Ginny answered. "He didn't want to have a *date* with me. I was just doing him a favor because his girlfriend was away."

"Sometimes, dates grow out of favors that people do for their friends," Mrs.

"Well, I'm not going steady,"
Ginny said unhappily.

Scott answered.

"Well, this favor didn't grow into anything," Ginny said. She jumped out of the chair and started pacing the floor. "I don't think I'm ever going to have a date, so I'll never even be able to *decide* whether to go steady or not."

"Maybe you'll meet some nice boys at the lake this year," her mother said.

"No, I won't," Ginny answered. "The only boys at the lake are two years old! Some vacation this will be."

Just then, the telephone rang. "I'll get it," Ginny said in a discouraged voice. "When the phone rings at Andrea's, it's some boy asking her out. This is probably somebody trying to sell us encyclopedias."

"Hello. Oh, hi, Tod," Ginny said. Mrs. Scott watched her daughter's face light up with a smile as she listened to Tod on the phone. "I had a good time at the Mancusos' party with you, too," Ginny told him.

"Oh... I'm sorry. I can't go out with you tomorrow night," Ginny said. "I'm leaving tomorrow morning for a two-week vacation."

Mrs. Scott sat forward in her chair listening. Ginny looked so disappointed. *It* would *have to happen just when we were going on vacation,* Mrs. Scott thought.

Then another big smile spread across Ginny's face. "That sounds great, Tod," she said. "I'd love to. I'll call you as soon as I get back from vacation."

That sounds promising, Mrs. Scott said to herself.

"You want the address there? Oh... yes, I would like to get a letter from you. Maybe I'll even write back," Ginny laughed. "The address is Silver Pines Cottage, Lake Mattawa, Orange, Massachusetts. See you soon. Good-by, Tod."

Ginny hung up the phone and danced excitedly around the living room. "My first 'real' date!" she exclaimed. "I'm going out in two weeks on my first 'real' date. I don't believe it! Tod invited me to go to Andrea's pool party with him when I get home from the lake."

Ginny ran over and hugged her mother. "He's going to write to me there, too. He said he had a *very* good time with me at the Mancusos' party. I just don't believe it!"

"I do," her mother answered. "You're a very lovely, nice, friendly girl. Any boy who didn't have a good time with you wouldn't be worth going out with anyway."

"Oh, Mom, you just think that

because you're my mother!" Ginny exclaimed. "That's not what that advice column would say."

"Well, you can't believe everything you read in the newspapers," her mother laughed.

"I'm going to pack for the lake now," Ginny announced happily. "Then maybe I'll write Tod a letter."

"You just finished talking to him a minute ago," her mother said in surprise. "Slow down, or you'll scare him away."

"That's all right. I won't mail it until I get his letter." Ginny skipped off to her bedroom to pack.

The next afternoon, the Scotts arrived at the lake in time for a nice cool swim before supper.

"This is the life!" Mr. Scott said as he floated in the water.

"It would be if there were any boys older than two within a hundred miles," Ginny answered.

"There's one now," her father said, pointing behind her.

Ginny didn't turn around. "Come on, Dad, you're a big tease!" Ginny laughed. She splashed her father.

"He's not bad-looking either," Mr. Scott replied. "He must be the son of those folks who rented the Roberts' cottage this year."

Ginny turned in time to see a tall, handsome boy dive off the dock into the water. In a few seconds, he surfaced right between Ginny and her parents.

"Hi," the boy said. "I'm Andy Stewart. My parents want to know if you would like to come to a barbecue at our cottage tonight so you don't have to cook and unpack, too."

"Hi," the boy said. "I'm Andy Stewart."

"That sounds great to me," Mr. Scott said. Mrs. Scott nodded. "I'm Jim Scott. This is my wife, Susan, and our daughter, Ginny. We would love to come to a barbecue at your cottage."

"Great!" Andy said, smiling at Ginny. "I'll go tell my parents. Would you like to go for a boat ride after supper, Ginny?" he asked.

"Yes, I'd like that," Ginny said.

"Good. See you later." Andy dived back under the water and swam to shore.

"The lake is looking a little bit more interesting now, isn't it?" Mr. Scott laughed and splashed his daughter.

"You might have your first 'real' date even before you go out with Tod," Mrs. Scott said. "And just one short day ago, you didn't believe me when I said you'd have a date sometime soon. Maybe I should write my own advice column.

What do you think of that?"

"Well . . . I'm not sure," Ginny said. She pretended to be concentrating very hard. "I suppose you were right about the date, and you may be right about going steady. But I still think you're wrong about one thing," Ginny giggled.

"What's that?" her mother asked.

"I don't think it's ever possible to have too many dates!"

Romeo on Roller Skates

Jack and Neal walked home from school in deep discussion. "Roller-skating! I've never been roller-skating in my life!" Neal said.

"Well, you've been ice-skating. It's the same thing, only warmer," Jack answered.

"I've only been ice-skating a couple of times, and I didn't do too well at that either," Neal laughed. "Why don't we do something *safe* — like bowling?"

"Next week, we'll go bowling. Tonight, let's go to the skating rink." Jack poked Neal in the ribs. "Come on," he said.

Neal shrugged his shoulders. "I don't know, Jack," he said.

"I heard that a lot of the girls from Ms. Harris' homeroom are going to be there," Jack tempted him.

"Is Linda Miller going?" Neal questioned.

"I think so," his friend answered.

"You've got me." Neal held up his arms in a gesture of surrender. "I'll be a real daredevil and go roller-skating."

"Just don't make me have to scrape you off the floor. I'm going to be too busy trying to make a date with Theresa

Buckley," Jack laughed.

"OK, I'll meet you tonight in front of the rink. I'll be the one with the helmet and the kneepads on," Neal joked as the two boys headed home in different directions.

Neal thought about Linda Miller as he walked the rest of the way home. *Maybe she'll be a terrible skater, too. Maybe she'll bump into me, and I'll have to hold on to her to help her stay up,* he imagined. *Then I'll ask her out.*

Neal had been interested in Linda since school started a few weeks ago, but she always seemed to be in the middle of a bunch of her own friends. He didn't know how to get to know her better without being too obvious.

That night, Neal was a little late getting to the skating rink. When he arrived, Jack said, "I was starting to think you weren't going to come!"

"Who, me?" Neal laughed. "Not on your life! I'm going to get a date with Linda Miller. I've got it all worked out." Jack and Neal went inside the skating rink.

"Tell me about this great plan for getting Linda to go out with you," Jack said. "Maybe I'll try it on Theresa Buckley."

"Well, Linda is going to be a terrible skater. She's going to bump into me, and . . . oh, no!" Neal groaned.

"What?"

"Look at her!" Neal pointed to Linda. She was skating backwards around the rink. She moved as smoothly past the other skaters as if she were a dancer.

"She can skate!" Neal exclaimed.

"Not only can she skate, it looks as if she's the best skater in the whole place,"

Jack laughed. "Well, Romeo, you're going to have to change your plans, because she's not going to bump into you!"

"Are you sure you don't want to go bowling?" Neal asked with a grin on his face.

"Put your skates on," Jack answered. "There's no backing out now."

Neal put on the rented skates. Then, holding on to the wall, he made his way from the bench to the skating floor. "This is going to be just great!" he said humorously to Jack. "I'm going to let go of this wall and skate right out into the middle of that crowd. I'll fall flat on my face. They are all going to skate right over me, and Linda Miller can come to my funeral. How about *that* for a plan?"

"Just great, Neal!" Jack answered. "That sounds more realistic than your first plan." He laughed at his friend and then skated out into the crowd circling the rink.

Neal inched his way forward, still hanging on to the wall. *This is ridiculous,* he thought to himself. *A five-foot, ten-inch first baseman reduced to a shivering mass of fear by a pair of roller skates!*

He moved slowly away from the wall. *Other people can do this. No more clowning around, Neal. Get out there,* he told himself. He moved a little bit faster, and suddenly, he was out of control. He lurched forward, swinging his arms like propellers. He half-slid and half-fell—right into the arms of Linda Miller!

"Hey, first-timer!" she said with a beautiful smile. "Hang on." She steadied him with her arms. "I'll help you get your balance for a few turns."

Just then, Jack skated by. "Way to

Suddenly, Neal was out of control.

go, Neal!" he said.

"I didn't plan this one!" Neal shouted after him.

"Plan?" Linda asked as they skated slowly forward together.

"Yes," Neal confessed. "I had it all planned that you were going to fall into *my* arms. You were going to be so grateful that I saved you from being run over by hordes of wild, roller-skating maniacs that you would agree to go out with me," Neal told her with a grin.

"Well, if I hadn't seen you almost fall with my own eyes, I'd be ready to believe this was a trick," Linda said with a laugh. "But nobody could have looked the way you did on purpose!"

Neal almost lost his balance trying to get out of the way of another skater. Linda held him up. They both started to laugh. "No," she said, "I don't think I'd better fall into your arms on the skating rink yet."

"You're right," he responded. "It would be crazy to fall into my arms while I'm on roller skates. But if you'll bring me to the bench, I can take off my skates in eight seconds flat. Then you're more than welcome to fall into my arms as often as you like," Neal said, smiling at her.

"The Romeo of the roller-skating rink!" Linda laughed. "You're so generous, but I want to skate now. I just got here a half-hour ago."

"I can wait," Neal answered.

"How long?"

"A couple of hours, a week, a year — however long it takes," he said, half-seriously.

"That sounds fair," Linda answered, with a twinkle in her eyes. "Why don't

"It couldn't be better if I'd planned it,"
Neal laughed.

we go out for a pizza tonight after the rink closes. We can decide then when the best time would be for me to fall into your arms," she said, giggling.

"That's the best idea I've heard all day," Neal answered. "It couldn't be better if I'd planned it," he laughed.

She smiled at him, and they skated on together, hand in hand, around the rink.

Even
Without
a Tan

Ann was sitting at the breakfast table thinking unhappily about her summer job. Today would be her first day at The Print Shop, the largest printing business in the area.

"I wish I'd never said I would take

that job this summer," Ann told her mother.

Mrs. Carlson sat down at the kitchen table opposite Ann. "Why, dear?" she asked. "I thought you wanted to earn money for art school—and get some art experience."

"None of my friends have to work," Ann complained.

"Your friends' families have a lot more money than we do," Ann's mother answered calmly. "But everybody has to work sometime. You'll just be getting a head start."

"I don't want a head start," Ann said. "I want to go to the lake with Betsy and Mary and Naomi. They'll get beautiful tans and meet lots of boys. I'll be as pale as a ghost and sit home every weekend with you and Dad."

Her mother started to laugh. "What a

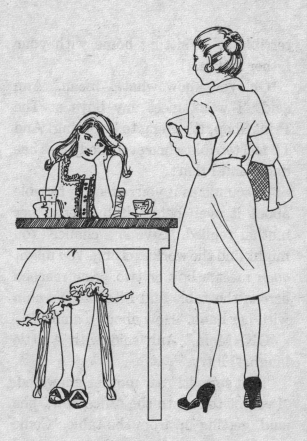

"I wish I'd never said I would take that job,"
Ann told her mother.

terrible fate — sitting home with your father and me!"

"Oh, you know what I mean," Ann said. "I won't meet any boys at The Print Shop. It's going to be boring! And I'll feel terrible when everybody else has dates and I don't."

"It sounds as if you're feeling terrible about it even before it happens," her mother replied. "Give it a chance. You might find the work exciting. You might *even* meet a boy or two." She reached across the table and lifted Ann's chin with her hand. "How about a smile?"

"OK, Mom," Ann said with a little laugh. "I'll try."

"That's great!" her mother answered. "I've got to run to the office now," she said, getting up from the table. "Come on. I'll drop you off at work on my way."

Mrs. Carlson drove through the morning commuter traffic. "Look at all these people going to work," she said to Ann.

"Yeah," Ann answered glumly. "But look at that handsome guy over there." She pointed to a tall, dark-haired boy walking down Main Street with a camera strap over his shoulder. "He's got a great tan already. I'll bet *he* doesn't have to work. He probably spends the day at the lake."

"And Betsy and Mary and Naomi are going to meet him and go out with him and his friends. And you'll be left to wither away at home, right?" her mother laughed.

Ann laughed, too. "I guess I don't sound very optimistic, do I?"

"No, dear, you don't," her mother answered. "Try again. Here we are at The Print Shop," she said, pulling over to the curb. "Keep your eyes open for opportunities. If your boss sees that you're good and that you really want to learn, I'm sure she'll give you some interesting things to work on."

"OK, Mom," Ann said, getting out of the car. "I'll be the best summer helper they have!"

"See you at supper, dear," her mother said and drove off to her own job.

Ann stood for a minute on the sidewalk in front of The Print Shop. She lifted her face to the early morning sun and concentrated on smiling. Then she opened the door and walked in to her first summer job.

Someone came up behind her. She turned to hold the door open and discovered the tall, handsome boy she and her mother had passed on the way to work. Ann smiled at him. He smiled back. *I wonder if he comes here often,*

Ann smiled at the boy.

she thought. *He's gorgeous!*

Ann's boss, Ms. Santana, saw her and walked over. "Good morning, Ann," she said. "And Bob. Great! You're both on time, so I'll give you the grand tour together before you start work."

I don't believe it! Ann thought. *This might turn out to be better than the lake after all.*

"Ann, this is Bob Zabak. Bob, meet Ann Carlson," Ms. Santana introduced them. She explained that Bob was going to be working in the Camera Department and that Ann would work in the Art Department.

Ann could feel Bob looking at her as Ms. Santana took them on a tour of The Print Shop. Her cheeks felt warm and flushed. Every once in a while, she sneaked a glance at him. *I hope he's as nice as he looks*, she thought.

All morning, as she was learning about her new job, Ann found herself thinking about Bob. *How can I get to know him better?* she wondered.

Just before lunch hour, Bob walked over to Ann's desk. He seemed a little nervous. "Ann, would you do me a big favor?" he asked. "This is a strange thing to ask since we've just met, but . . ." He paused.

"I'd be happy to do you a favor," Ann answered. "What is it?"

He probably wants me to give him a ride to work, she thought. *Well, that's better than nothing.*

"I'm getting a portfolio ready for photography school. I'd love to take your picture in the park at lunchtime."

"That's fine," she answered, trying to appear calm. "I was planning to eat my lunch in the park today anyway."

"Great!" he answered. "I'll meet you at noon, then."

Ann could hardly believe what she was hearing. She felt her cheeks flush. She kept wanting to smile.

At the park, Bob took some pictures of Ann with flowers held up to her face to smell, with flowers in her hair, and with flowers in her lap as she sat on the grass. While he was taking the pictures, Ann kept thinking, *I hope I look all right.*

Bob kept thinking, *This girl is beautiful!*

When he was through taking photographs, Bob said, "I'd like to bring you some flowers this weekend. Will you go out with me on Saturday night?"

Ann nodded her head. She was so happy she could hardly speak.

When Ann got home for supper, she

*Bob took pictures of Ann with flowers held up
to her face.*

was still feeling wonderful. She said to her mother, "Remember how terrible I felt this morning?"

"I certainly do," her mother answered.

"You wouldn't believe the day I had!" Ann said. "I like my job. And that handsome guy we saw this morning works at The Print Shop. He took my picture today with some flowers, and he asked me out for this weekend. He likes me— even without a tan!" Ann waltzed around the kitchen happily.

"Imagine that," Mrs. Carlson said with a grin. "Even without a tan!" And she laughed as Ann danced around the room.

The Saturday Night Date

I'm babysitting for the third Saturday night in a row! It's enough to make a girl lose confidence in herself, Carol thought.

Carol was babysitting for the Dalton's two children. They were finally asleep. Now Carol was standing in the hallway of their apartment looking at herself in the big mirror on the wall.

"If you looked like Maria, you'd have a date tonight," she said to her reflection. She pulled her long brown hair back from her face and braided it. *I wonder if I could wear my hair the way Maria does,* Carol thought. *No, my neck looks too long.* She let her hair fall to her shoulders.

Just then, she heard someone outside the apartment door. *The Daltons can't be home yet,* she thought. *It's much too early.* She heard a key turning in the lock. The door opened as far as the safety chain would let it. *It must be the Daltons,* Carol thought, moving to let them in. Then she heard a strange male voice.

"Hey," the voice called. "Unlock the door."

Carol thought for a second that she was going to faint. Thinking quickly, she threw herself against the door, slamming it shut.

The voice called again, "Hey, come on. Let me in!"

Carol didn't say a word. She just pushed as hard as she could against the door. Her heart was pounding. She heard the key turning in the lock again and felt the door being pushed open slightly.

"No more fooling around, kids!" the voice said. "Let me in, or I'm going to call Mom."

Mom? Carol thought. *What's going on?* The chain was straining to hold the door. "Go away, or I'll call the police," Carol said to the person in the hall.

"Who are you?" the voice answered in surprise.

"Go away, or I'll call the police," Carol said.

"Who are *you?*" Carol asked.

"Pete Dalton," the voice said. "Let me in. I live here."

"No, you don't," Carol insisted. "You've got the wrong apartment."

"Say, are you a babysitter?" the voice said.

"Yes," Carol answered, "but the Daltons will be back any minute." This wasn't true, but Carol wanted to scare the stranger away.

"Look," the voice said, "I'm sorry I scared you. I *am* Pete Dalton. Tommy and Jeff are my brothers. I go to the university. That's why you've never met me."

"Well, why didn't your parents tell me you were coming home tonight?" Carol asked suspiciously.

"They didn't know. I came to surprise them on their anniversary tomorrow," the voice answered.

It is *their anniversary tomorrow,* Carol thought. She felt an enormous sense of relief. Carol moved away from the door and looked out through the open space. She saw a tall, handsome boy with dark red hair. A suitcase was on the floor beside him. He wasn't pushing the door anymore.

"How can I be sure you're Pete Dalton?" she asked.

"You can wake up the kids," he said with a big smile. "Or you can get a photograph album from the living-room bookshelf. There are some pictures of me in there."

She ran into the living room and came back with an album. She flipped through the pages, looking back and forth from the photographs to the boy in the doorway. "OK," she said, "I believe you."

"Thank heavens!" he answered with a grin. "Now may I come in?"

"Yes," Carol said, smiling. She unlocked the chain and opened the door wide.

"Hi," Pete said, holding out his hand. "I'm sorry I frightened you. You handled the situation very well though. I'm glad my brothers have a babysitter like you."

Carol shook hands with Pete. "Thanks," she said. "And I'm glad you're not what I was afraid you were."

"I am, too," Pete said seriously. "I hope I haven't wrecked my chance forever to make a good impression on you."

"No, of course you haven't," Carol answered. She smiled up at him. "Come on in. I was just going to make popcorn and listen to some music. Will you join me?"

"I'd like that," he answered.

They went into the kitchen, where

Pete helped her make the popcorn. He told her about the university and how much he liked it. His eyes were bright with enthusiasm as he spoke.

Carol enjoyed listening to him. *I wish he still lived at home,* she thought. *I'd dye my hair black like Maria's if it would make him want to go out with me.*

When the popcorn was ready, they took it into the living room and put a record on the stereo. "Now tell me about yourself," Pete said.

He smiled at her, and she thought she would melt. She told him about high school, about playing tennis and studying music. She felt very comfortable talking with him.

"You do some interesting things," Pete said. "There's something that puzzles me, though."

"Yes?" Carol asked.

"Why is a lovely girl like you baby-sitting on a Saturday night?" he questioned. "Why isn't the hallway littered with guys fighting for the chance to take you out?"

Carol laughed and blushed at the same time. "I don't know," she answered softly.

"I don't either," Pete said, shaking his head in amazement. "Well, I'm here, and I'd like to take you out, Carol. Will you consider this a date and dance with me?"

Carol nodded her head and got up. Pete took her in his arms. They moved slowly around the floor to soft saxophone music.

He held her tighter. "Your hair smells as beautiful as it looks," he said. "I'm really glad the guys around here are too stupid to have asked you out for tonight."

She tilted her head up at him. "I am,

too, Pete," she said. "I'm having a wonderful time."

Just then, they heard a key in the front door. "Another intruder?" Pete asked.

"No," said Carol, looking at her watch. "It's your parents." She was very disappointed. *I'll never see him again,* she thought.

"Darn it," Pete said. "I didn't want this date to end."

Mr. and Mrs. Dalton were thrilled to see Pete and very pleased to hear how Carol had reacted to his arrival. Mrs. Dalton paid Carol for babysitting, and her husband was about to walk her to her apartment when Pete said, "It's all right, Dad. I'll see Carol home. I want to have time to persuade her to come up to the university next weekend and have a *real* date with me."

*"Pete," Carol said, "I'm having a
wonderful time."*

Carol felt a glow all through her body.

"You mean you'd take our favorite babysitter?" his father asked with a grin.

"If she'll let me," Pete answered, and he ushered Carol out into the hall.

I don't need to look like Maria, she thought. *He likes me just as I am.* She looked up at Pete happily. *This is the best Saturday night date of my life!*